DEC 1 4 2020

jE DEALEY Erin
Dear Earth... :from your
friends in Room 5 /
Dealey, Erin,

WITHDRAWN

D0574346

Dear Earth...

From Your Friends in Room 5

Erin Dealey Luisa Uribe

HARPER
An Imprint of HarperCollinsPublishers

To Earth Heroes everywhere, with special thanks to Tamar Mays and Deborah Warren—E. D.

Para mi mamá, con un abrazo—L. U.

Dear Earth . . . From Your Friends in Room 5. Text copyright © 2020 by Erin Dealey. Illustrations copyright © 2020 by Luisa Uribe. All rights reserved. Manufactured in Italy. No part of this book may be used or reproduced in any manner whatsoever without written permission except in the case of brief quotations embodied in critical articles and reviews.
For information address HarperCollins Children's Books, a division of HarperCollins Publishers, 195 Broadway, New York, NY 10007. www.harpercollinschildren.com
Library of Congress Control Number: 2019956220
ISBN 978-0-06-291532-0
The artist used Photoshop to create the digital illustrations for this book.
Typography by Erica De Chavez. 20 21 22 23 24 RTLO 10 9 8 7 6 5 4 3 2 1 ❖ First Edition

Dear Earth, JANUARY

Happy New Year! We're making resolutions.
(We hope that this note reaches you.)
THANK YOU for all that you give to our world.
We'd like to do our part too.
How can we help?

Sincerely,
Room 5

Dear Room 5,

Your letter arrived on the wind.
A whisper of hope in the night.
I'm thankful for helpers who care for their planet.
Here's one way: please turn off the lights.
Using less electricity saves energy.
Stargazers will thank you too!

Your friend,
Earth

THANK YOU!

FEBRUARY

Dear Earth,

We unplugged our chargers and turned off our lights.

Some of us even saw stars.

This month we're charting how much we use plastic.

OH MY—plastic trash travels so far!

Sincerely,

Room 5

P.S. Check out our reusable water bottles. No more single-use bottles or straws for us.

Dear Room 5,

The stars in the universe thank you.

Our friends in the ocean will too.

Some turtles and fish mistake plastic for dinner!

Does that sound nutritious to you?

Your friend,

Earth

MARCH

Dear Earth,

Blech!

We sure wouldn't want to eat plastic.

(Bernard says he might, but he's teasing.)

We're sprouting seeds for a vegetable garden.

We'll plant when the weather's not FREEZING.

Soon . . . we hope!

Sincerely,

Room 5

Dear Room 5,

Springtime does seem rather fickle.

The reasons have caused big debates.

My climate is tricky, but YOU keep me hopeful.

What's next on your list? I can't wait!

Your friend,

Earth

Dear Earth,

APRIL

We learned about climate change. (Yikes!)
We've planted some trees. Aren't they cool?
And now that it's April, our whole class decided
we're biking or walking to school.

Sincerely,
Your friends in Room 5

P.S. Did you notice we wrote this on recycled paper? We are trying to use both sides of our paper when we can.

Dear Room 5,

I'm proud of your efforts year-round.
Some people just help on Earth Day.
(Which is fine!)
I'm going to call you Earth Heroes
instead of Room 5—
Do you mind?

Forever grateful,
Earth

MAY

Dear Earth,

WOW!

We'll happily be your Earth Heroes.

(Bernard wants a cape or some wings . . .)

Plus, we won't be "Room 5" this summer,

and who knows what next year will bring?

Proudly,

Your Earth Heroes

P.S. We planted the garden!

Dear Earth Heroes,

My glorious friends—

I hope you'll still help when school's out.

Be water-smart washers, teeth brushers, and bathers.

Save water in wet years or drought.

(Tell Bernard this does not get him out of showering . . .)

Your friend,

Earth

JUNE

Dear Earth,

Happy summer! No school!

We promise to try and save water.

(I won't splash so much at the pool.)

And I'm not playing video games or watching TV—

well, not as much anyway . . .

Guess what?

My dad and I are going camping.

Hope I see some stars.

I'm not very good at rhyming.

Your friend,

Bernard

Dear Bernard,

Summer is a great time for camping.

Go explore. Run and play. Boat or hike.

Thank you for keeping the Earth Heroes going.

Share these summer ideas if you like:

- Clean up beaches and playgrounds
- Shop at a local farmers market
- Compost

Your friend,
Earth

P.S. If you can, look for times when your family might turn down the air conditioner. It uses a lot of electricity!

SEPTEMBER

Dear Earth,

We did all the things you suggested.

The vegetable garden looks great!

It's still out behind our old classroom.

(Now most of us are in Room 8.)

And the Earth Heroes rule!

It's our new club at school.

Guess who's writing this?

Bernard, Earth Heroes President

P.S. For September, we're asking the cafeteria to use less plastic. They're already adding our food scraps from lunch to the compost. Boy, those worms in our garden will be happy!

Dear Earth Heroes,

I'm so glad to hear from my friends.

(Bernard—Look at YOU. You're a poet!)

Even better, you're all taking care of our home.

Am I proud of my Heroes? You know it!

Welcome back!

—Earth

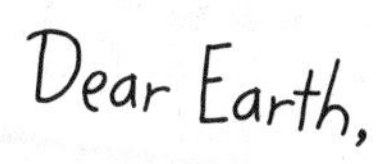

OCTOBER

Dear Earth,

We're getting creative
for our school's annual costume parade.
There are prizes for costumes from recycled junk.
Three guesses what Pres. Bernard made?

Your wacky friends,
The Earth Heroes

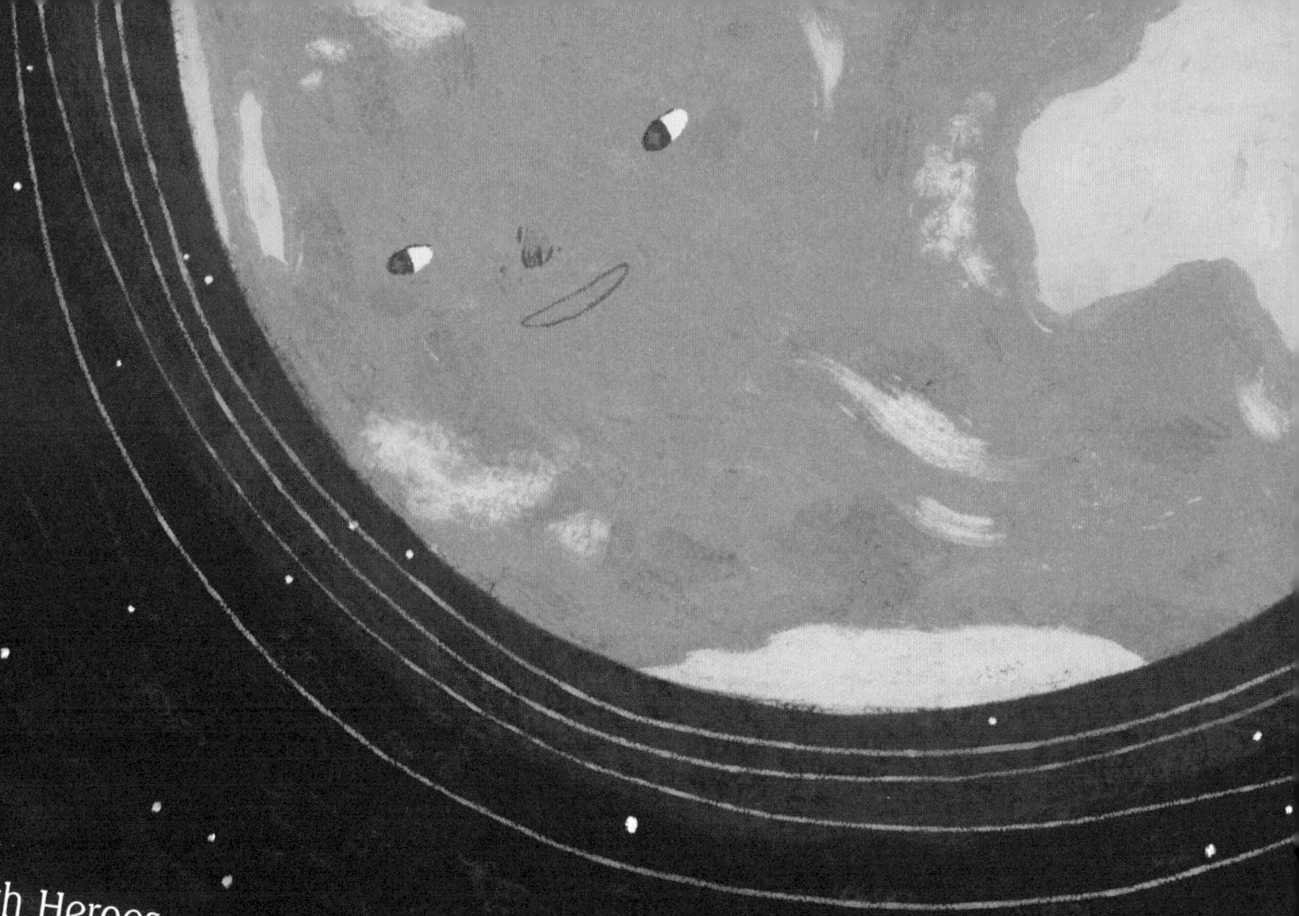

Dear Earth Heroes,

Your spirit is certainly growing.
Here's to making new stuff from old things.
You've reused, reduced, and recycled.
And Bernard, what incredible wings!
What are you planning for November?

Your fan,
Earth

NOVEMBER

Dear Earth,

The Earth Heroes ARE growing!

Our club now has seven new members.

This month (and always) we are thankful for YOU,

and we're sharing our food in November.

With thanks,

The Earth Heroes

Dear Earth Heroes,

My heart soars with every letter.
I'm thankful to be in good hands.
I wish I could show you
what a difference you're making.
I'm truly your #1 fan.

—Earth

DECEMBER

Dear Earth,

Season's Greetings!

We made decorations from paper-towel tubes.

We're regifting presents this year.

We've wrapped them with recycled ribbons and paper.

We wish you a **Happy Earth Year**!

Love always,

Your Earth Heroes

Dear Earth Heroes,

Thank you for caring!
Our world needs more heroes like you.
Pass it on. Keep it going.
Please never stop showing
the good things Earth Heroes can do!
I'll be watching . . .

Your #1 fan,
Earth

Dear Earth Heroes—

THANK YOU for knowing how important it is to save Earth. Want to learn more?

Millions of years ago, way before dinosaurs, fuels formed from fossils of dead plants and animals. When we use electricity, heat or cool our homes, or drive around town, we use *energy* from oil, coal, and natural gas—made from those *fossil fuels.*

Using fossil fuels releases certain gases into the air. In limited amounts, these gases help keep Earth's temperature just right. However, when large amounts of these gases are released, they trap the sun's heat—like the air in a balloon—instead of allowing the heat to escape into space.

Can you picture Earth in the center of that balloon? The wind and ocean currents move the trapped heat around Earth, warming the air, water, and soil in some areas and cooling others. Warmer air melts our glaciers, raising sea levels; flooding coastal towns, beaches, and marshes; and harming habitats of coastal birds, fish, and wildlife!

Thank goodness scientists have been working on creating *renewable* energy from solar, water, and wind. This will reduce our need of *nonrenewable* fossil fuels. (The ones that can't be replaced once they are used up.)

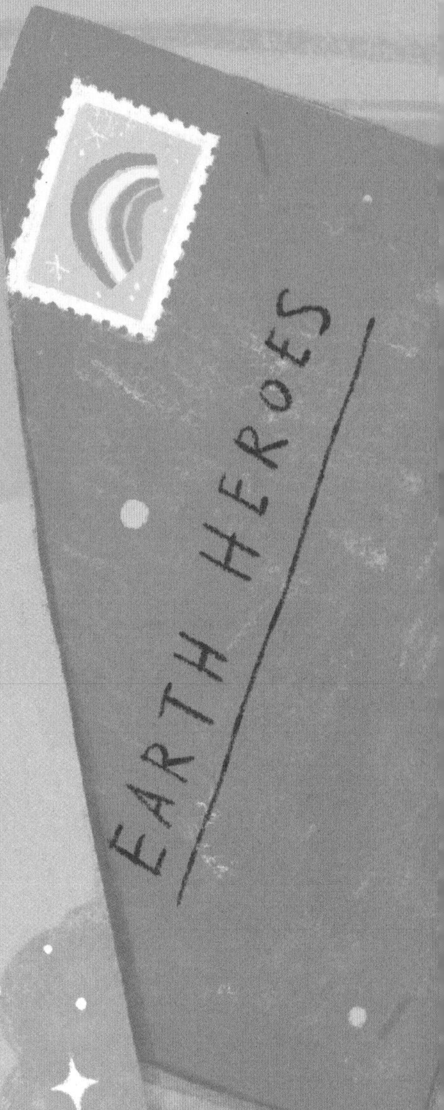

Kids like YOU have the power to make a difference.
Join the club. Or start your own! Take the
Earth Hero Pledge:

I promise to do my best
To be an Earth Hero,
Protect our environment, and
Respect the world we live in.

Earth Heroes can help too! How?
Here are four important R words:

Reduce: *Using less energy* will save fossil fuels. Walk to school, bike, or carpool. Turn off lights and unplug electrical devices that aren't in use. Turn off the faucet while you brush your teeth or wash your hands.

Earth Heroes can *reduce* the use of plastic (which is made from fossil fuels) by ordering drinks without a straw at restaurants.

Recycle: *Let's change the trash cycle.* Make art out of old junk, scraps, and wire. Get creative, Earth Heroes! Turn your favorite birthday or holiday cards into gift tags.

How about helping your family start a compost bin? Add plant prunings or leaves, grass cuttings, vegetable or fruit waste, tea bags, and more. Your garden will love it!

Reuse: *Using things more than once* creates less trash. Plus, energy was used to create every item you throw away. Buy something new, and the trash cycle will continue. Yikes!

Reusable cloth bags can replace plastic bags at the store. Bring reusable water bottles to school or practice. Use both sides of your paper to save trees and water.

Renew: *Make things like new again.* Earth Heroes can help renew our environment by cleaning up beaches, riverbanks, and playgrounds.

Composting not only recycles old waste, it helps to renew Earth's soil. So does planting a tree. Yep. Those pretty trees that give us shade also help absorb those fossil fuel gases and refresh our air by producing oxygen. Wow!

I'm already so very proud of YOU! Your friend, Erin Dealey

I PROMISE TO DO MY BEST
PROTECT OUR ENVIRONMENT
EARTH HERO
RESPECT THE WORLD WE LIVE IN
TO BE AN EARTH HERO
EARTH HEROES
Endange
Species
WILDFLOWERS
OREGA
water: fridays
compost: every
* other day*